THE TALE OF

MR. JEREMY FISHER

BY

BEATRIX POTTER

Author of
" The Tale of Peter Rabbit," &c.

BLOOMSBURY BOOKS
in association with
FREDERICK WARNE

BLOOMSBURY BOOKS IN ASSOCIATION WITH FREDERICK WARNE

Published by the Penguin Group
Penguin Books Ltd, 27 Wrights Lane, London W8 5TZ, England
Penguin Books USA Inc., 375 Hudson Street, New York, N.Y. 10014, USA
Penguin Books Australia Ltd, Ringwood, Victoria, Australia
Penguin Books Canada Ltd, 10 Alcorn Avenue, Toronto, Ontario, Canada M4V 3B2
Penguin Books (N.Z.) Ltd, 182-190 Wairau Road, Auckland 10, New Zealand

Penguin Books Ltd, Registered Offices: Harmondsworth, Middlesex, England

Bloomsbury Books, an imprint of The Godfrey Cave Group,
42 Bloomsbury Street, London WC1B 3QJ

First published by Frederick Warne & Co. 1906
Published with new reproductions 1987
This edition first published 1993

ISBN 1 85471 360 4

Printed and bound in Great Britain by
William Clowes Limited, Beccles and London

FOR
STEPHANIE
FROM
COUSIN B.

8

ONCE upon a time there was a frog called Mr. Jeremy Fisher; he lived in a little damp house amongst the buttercups at the edge of a pond.

THE water was all slippy-sloppy in the larder and in the back passage.

But Mr. Jeremy liked getting his feet wet; nobody ever scolded him, and he never caught a cold!

11

12

HE was quite pleased when he looked out and saw large drops of rain, splashing in the pond—

"I WILL get some worms and go fishing and catch a dish of minnows for my dinner," said Mr. Jeremy Fisher. "If I catch more than five fish, I will invite my friends Mr. Alderman Ptolemy Tortoise and Sir Isaac Newton. The Alderman, however, eats salad."

15

16

MR. JEREMY put on a macintosh, and a pair of shiny goloshes; he took his rod and basket, and set off with enormous hops to the place where he kept his boat.

THE boat was round and
green, and very like the
other lily-leaves. It was
tied to a water-plant in
the middle of the pond.

19

MR. JEREMY took a reed
pole, and pushed the
boat out into open water. "I
know a good place for minnows," said Mr. Jeremy
Fisher.

M<small>R.</small> JEREMY stuck his pole into the mud and fastened his boat to it.

Then he settled himself cross-legged and arranged his fishing tackle. He had the dearest little red float. His rod was a tough stalk of grass, his line was a fine long white horse-hair, and he tied a little wriggling worm at the end.

23

THE rain trickled down his back, and for nearly an hour he stared at the float.

"This is getting tiresome, I think I should like some lunch," said Mr. Jeremy Fisher.

HE punted back again amongst the water-plants, and took some lunch out of his basket.

"I will eat a butterfly sandwich, and wait till the shower is over," said Mr. Jeremy Fisher.

A GREAT big water-beetle came up underneath the lily leaf and tweaked the toe of one of his goloshes.

Mr. Jeremy crossed his legs up shorter, out of reach, and went on eating his sandwich.

ONCE or twice something
moved about with a
rustle and a splash amongst
the rushes at the side of the
pond.

"I trust that is not a rat,"
said Mr. Jeremy Fisher; " I
think I had better get away
from here."

32

MR. JEREMY shoved the boat out again a little way, and dropped in the bait. There was a bite almost directly; the float gave a tremendous bobbit!

"A minnow! a minnow! I have him by the nose!" cried Mr. Jeremy Fisher, jerking up his rod.

BUT what a horrible surprise! Instead of a smooth fat minnow, Mr. Jeremy landed little Jack Sharp the stickleback, covered with spines!

35

36

THE stickleback floundered about the boat, pricking and snapping until he was quite out of breath. Then he jumped back into the water.

AND a shoal of other little fishes put their heads out, and laughed at Mr. Jeremy Fisher.

40

AND while Mr. Jeremy sat disconsolately on the edge of his boat—sucking his sore fingers and peering down into the water—a *much* worse thing happened; a really *frightful* thing it would have been, if Mr. Jeremy had not been wearing a macintosh!

A GREAT big enormous trout came up—ker-pflop-p-p-p! with a splash—and it seized Mr. Jeremy with a snap, "Ow! Ow! Ow!"—and then it turned and dived down to the bottom of the pond!

43

44

BUT the trout was so displeased with the taste of the macintosh, that in less than half a minute it spat him out again; and the only thing it swallowed was Mr. Jeremy's goloshes.

MR. JEREMY bounced up
to the surface of the
water, like a cork and the
bubbles out of a soda water
bottle; and he swam with
all his might to the edge of
the pond.

47

48

HE scrambled out on the first bank he came to, and he hopped home across the meadow with his mac- intosh all in tatters.

"WHAT a mercy that was not a pike!" said Mr. Jeremy Fisher. "I have lost my rod and basket; but it does not much matter, for I am sure I should never have dared to go fishing again!"

51

52

HE put some sticking
plaster on his fingers,
and his friends both came to
dinner. He could not offer
them fish, but he had something else in his larder.

S IR ISAAC NEWTON
wore his black and gold
waistcoat,

55

AND Mr. Alderman Ptolemy
Tortoise brought a salad
with him in a string bag.

57

AND instead of a nice dish of minnows—they had a roasted grasshopper with lady-bird sauce; which frogs consider a beautiful treat; but *I* think it must have been nasty!

THE END